S0-AWS-915

On Monday, Alfred C. Dunphee woke up to his 100th birthday. Mr. D. said to his dog, "Pup, it's time to make some changes. You are only one hundred once."

Pup cocked an ear at Mr. D. who said, "First things first, old friend, I'll call ahead to the bakery while you run down there. We'll start the day with a celebration. A birthday cake!!"

The best thing about Mr. Dunphee's house was that he had everything he needed. Whatever he wanted, it was lost or hidden away in a cabinet or drawer, a box, a closet or in the basement. Mr. D. saved *everything!* So, instant decorations for a birthday party were right there! And, he had collections — stacks and stacks of books, so many clothes there were not enough days to wear them all, and his hat collection... 147 hats to be exact. There was a music collection, a magazine collection, a stamp collection. Mr. Dunphee had so many collections, he had not seen some of them for 33 years.

As they were eating gooey things from the Bakery, Mr. D. noticed Pup counting the candles. "Say, Pup, when will we put that many candles on your birthday cake?" They puzzled that together. Pup was 3 months old when Mr. D. found him and they have lived together for 13 years. "That means you are about 91 in dog years."

Pup barked. "Right," said Mr. D., "we'll have your 100th birthday party two or three months after my 101st birthday." They blew party horns at each other, counted the bakery boxes stacked in piles all over the house and counted their blessings at being 91 and 100.

By 4:00 that birthday afternoon, Mr. Dunphee made good his promise to make changes. Humming all the time, he and Pup carried out all the bakery boxes saved over the years. As they looked at the mountain of white boxes tied with red string in the driveway, Pup thought, too many to count. Mr. D. said, "Too many to save."

Tim and Amanda, neighbor kids, rode by on their bikes and yelled at Mr. Dunphee, "Good thing all the trash men are late today, Mr. D."

Mr. Dunphee and Pup lived in the smallest house in Midvale, Illinois. It was also the most careworn and faded. It desperately needed painting. Over the years, houses that were larger and finer had been built around him by people who were better able to take care of their houses.

Across the street in a large house lived Mr. and Mrs. Up & Over. They were the two people who were most critical of Mr. D. and his tattered house. They had even gone to the town council to complain.

Just before he went to bed each night, Mr. Dunphee went to his window and smiled at his neighbors across the street before closing the curtains. He and Pup went to sleep the night of his 100th birthday with even bigger smiles on their faces. What a wonderful day!!

On Tuesday morning, Mr. Dunphee said to Pup,
"Those changes felt so good, I want to make more today."

Pup cocked an ear. "Right," said Mr. D., "one of the things we are
going to do today is change your name. I mean, no dog who is 91
should have a name like Pup. Let's look in our books for a new one."
Mr. D. put on his slippers and went to the bookshelf.

By 4:00 that afternoon, Mr. Dunphee's driveway was a mountain of books. As he looked at his accomplishment, his life felt lighter. He has saved only 17 books for himself.

Amanda and Tim rode by and stopped to look at the books. "Say," said Amanda, "I'll bet they would like to have some of these books at the Library!" Pup, whose new name was Rover, was happy too. His new name had been selected from a series of books Mr. D. had loved called The Rover Boys.

Mr. and Mrs. Up & Over were on their front lawn, making plans to report Mr. D. for littering the neighborhood. Tim said they would ride to the Library to get someone to come and save the books.

Mr. Dunphee and Rover woke on Wednesday to some new ideas. Mr. D. felt that he was only part way through the changes in his life. "You know, Rover," he said, "there's good sense in not having things one doesn't need. I'll bet that *you* can see we really have too much." Rover barked in agreement. "I can see now that the things I own, really own me, rather than *them* belonging to me... let's get started, we are going to create another mountain today."

So, it was Mr. D.'s hat collection that made the newest mountain in front of their old and worn house. 147 hats in all, some with phrases written on them like *Over 60 and Loving It*, *Laguna Beach Forever* and *I don't care, either!*

Mr. D. was disappointed on Thursday morning. It was a rainy day. He and Rover had been undecided how today should be celebrated. After all, you are only 100 once and a person needs to make a birthday last as long as possible. They had thought they might create another mountain of Mr. D.'s collections, or they might have a picnic in the Park and run and play. The rain seemed to have ruined that.

The seventeen saved books were stacked neatly on the dresser. Rover was wearing his favorite collar and looking out the window. Water is dripping into the garage. The roof is leaking!

They rushed out to the garage and stood in the water coming down through the roof. It was fun, as if it was raining inside and out. Rover ran round and round chasing his tail as if he were 9 not 91.

After they raided the kitchen to put a bowl or pan underneath every drip and drop, Mr. D. said, "I have an idea." Rover barked. "Do you remember my collection of old license plates? Instead of throwing them away, why not make a new roof for the garage with them."

Rover wagged his tail and raced for the basement.

As they were carrying stacks and stacks of license plates to the garage, Tim and Amanda came over. "What are you going to do with *those*, Mr. D.?" "Make a new roof," said Mr. Dunphee. Amanda and Tim exchanged weird looks. "Can we help?" Rover barked happily. "There's your answer," said Mr. D.

Mr D. recalled all the places he had been to collect these license plates: Wyoming and Florida, Vermont and Tennessee, Washington State and Washington D.C. Even Alaska. Mr. Dunphee could not remember why he had many smaller plates that fit on the back of a motorcycle.

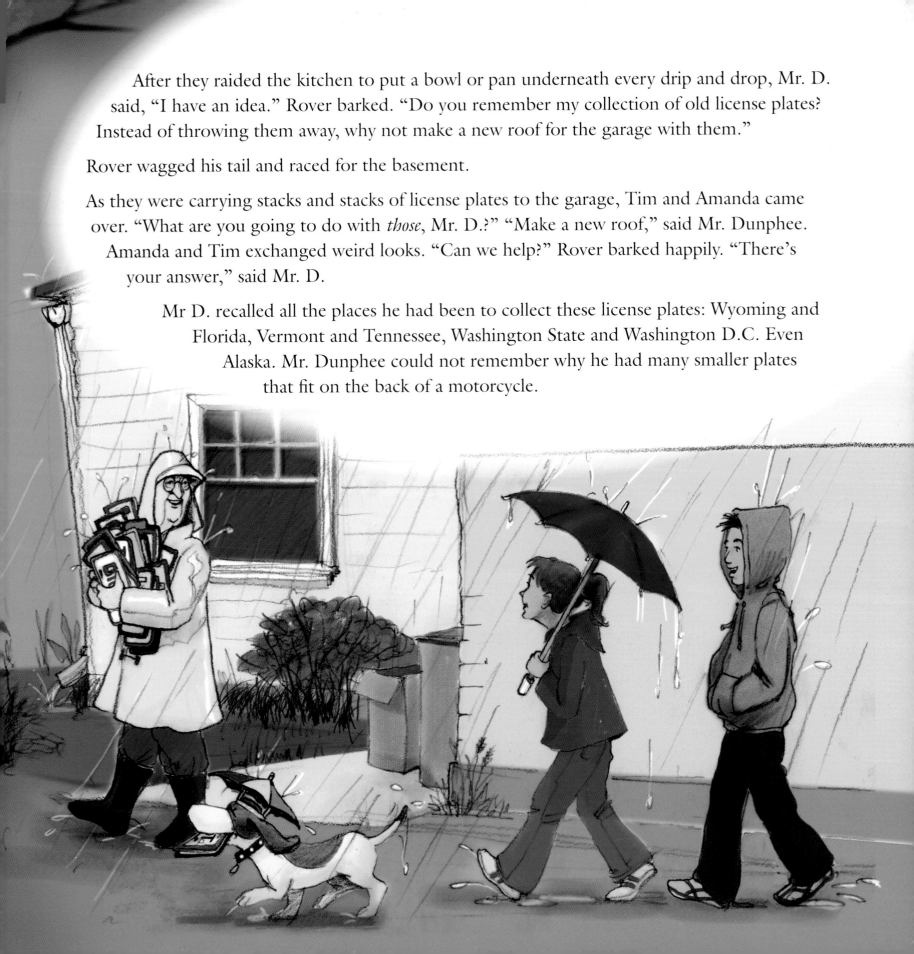

On Friday, the sun cooperated. It cleared away the clouds to watch Mr. Dunphee, Tim and Amanda carefully placing the license plates over the worn shingles. It was going to be a colorful garage and a good place for Mr. D's license plate collection. He was pleased that it would be useful.

From where he stood, Rover could see that this garage would be different and fun.

From where they stood, Mr. and Mrs. Up & Over were horrified and called City Hall to lodge a complaint: "It is unthinkable," they said, "that a garage in their neighborhood would have a roof of ugly old license plates." The clerk at City Hall said he would file paperwork that would result in a meeting next Monday with Mr. D. and the people from City Hall to talk about the appearance of his garage.

When they got up on Saturday, Mr. D. and Rover went outside to look at the garage. They agreed it was lovely. But, now they could see that the house looked very *plain*. What could they do to make the house more interesting, more like the garage?

Almost all Mr. Dunphee's collections had been used or given away. He still had his stamp collection but it was fragile. Besides, Mr. D. still liked to look at it and dream of faraway places.

"There must be something we have overlooked," Mr. Dunphee said after lunch. "Let's go down in the basement again." Rover ran down first.

The basement seemed a treasure cave with light streaming in the small windows. Rover remembered the storage closet which was always locked because the key was lost. He barked at Mr. Dunphee. "I hate keys," said Mr. D.

Mr. D. found a small metal bar and pried the door open. Inside they found the answer to all their wishes. Pennies, pennies and more pennies. Hundreds of them. It was Mr. Dunphee's old penny collection!

"Now," said Mr. D., "we know what to do, don't we?" Just as Rover barked, there was a tapping on the window. It was Amanda and Tim.

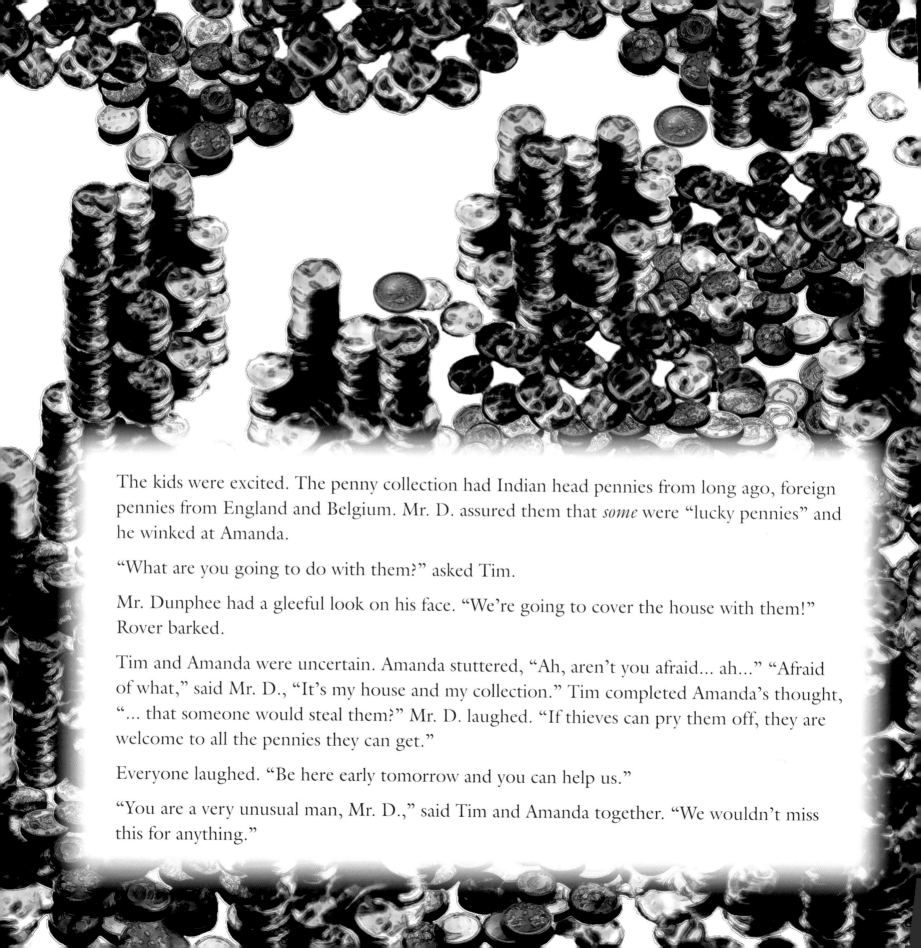

The kids were excited. The penny collection had Indian head pennies from long ago, foreign pennies from England and Belgium. Mr. D. assured them that *some* were "lucky pennies" and he winked at Amanda.

"What are you going to do with them?" asked Tim.

Mr. Dunphee had a gleeful look on his face. "We're going to cover the house with them!" Rover barked.

Tim and Amanda were uncertain. Amanda stuttered, "Ah, aren't you afraid... ah..." "Afraid of what," said Mr. D., "It's my house and my collection." Tim completed Amanda's thought, "... that someone would steal them?" Mr. D. laughed. "If thieves can pry them off, they are welcome to all the pennies they can get."

Everyone laughed. "Be here early tomorrow and you can help us."

"You are a very unusual man, Mr. D.," said Tim and Amanda together. "We wouldn't miss this for anything."

On Sunday, Mr. & Mrs. Up & Over looked out their window and were horrified even more than before. Mr. Up & Over put on his robe and ran across the street. "What are you doing to this house?" he cried. Mr. D. told him their artful plan. "But, we are having a party tonight for our important friends. They will be shocked." said Mr. U. & O.

Mr. Dunphee looked at the kids. "Do you think we can cover the house with pennies by dinnertime, so that Mr. Up & Over won't be embarrassed by our unfinished house?" Rover barked and jumped up and down. "There's your answer... we'll work hard, Mr. Up & Over."

Mr. Up & Over stomped across the street to tell his wife about the house being covered with pennies.

Tim and Amanda were puzzled. How could anyone *not* want to live across the street from a house covered with pennies?

The copper in the pennies caught the moonlight and made it glow as if it were a house of magic.

"Thanks for letting us help you, Mr. D.," Tim said. Amanda gave him a kiss on the cheek. Mr. D.'s eyes glowed with excitement. How beautiful, he thought, the perfect end to a birthday week.

Rover looked up at Mr. D. "When was the last time we slept out in the backyard? Not since you were a Pup." Rover barked. "Right," agreed Mr. D., "tomorrow is Monday. We can watch the moon set tonight, and then the sun rise in the morning over our shiny new house."

In the morning, all those invited to the meeting to discuss Mr. Dunphee's newly decorated house arrived.

The Police came.

The Town Council came.

Mr. and Mrs. Up & Over walked across the street.

When Mr. D. and Rover heard the voices, they got out of their pup tent and looked around the corner of the house. There was a crowd in the front yard. They thought these neighbors had come to admire their beautiful home.

No one noticed the family with the Michigan license plates on their car. They were just about to leave Midvale when they passed Penny House — that's what they called it. They were so amazed and delighted they had to stop to admire this unique home.

Before the meeting could get started, the visitors from Michigan introduced themselves to Mr. Up & Over, thinking he was the Mayor because he acted so important. They asked if the meeting on the front yard was to declare Penny House — that's what they called it — a Historic Home and Landmark, so it would always be here for visitors to come and behold.

The children from the Michigan family wondered how many pennies it took to cover a house, and how many dollars' worth were there. "This house is a treasure," said the mother from Michigan, "the people of Midvale, Illinois are lucky to have such good neighbors as Mr. Dunphee and Rover. We're going to tell all our friends to come here and visit."

The real Mayor of Midvale and the City Historian called a hasty conference with the Town Council and decided, then and there, to convey Historic Status for Penny House owned by Mr. Alfred C. Dunphee and Rover.

This way, it would be there for visitors to Midvale as well as its citizens... forever.

Rover barked. He would have plenty of time to wonder what changes he might make in his life when he became one hundred. He looked at Mr. D. and thought, you are only 100 once.

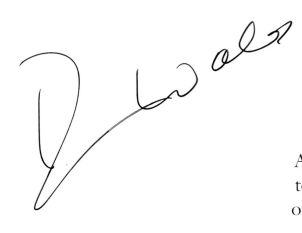

Penny House

Written by Dirk Wales
Illustrated by Diane Kenna

After you read Penny House, we hope you'll want
to make a "penny house" of your own with paper
or cardboard, crayons or paints. Glue pennies on it
to remind you that you should collect pennies
but not a lot of "stuff".

And, don't forget, you are only _____ once.
(your age here)

GREAT PLAINS PRESS

ISBN# 0-9632459-1-0
Published by Great Plains Press
118 North Aberdeen Street
Chicago, Illinois 60607
fax 773-525-6278 or 312-850-0033

©copyright 2005   All rights reserved.

Printed in China

10 9 8 7 6 5 4 3 2 1